The Eumenides

The Eumenides
Aeschylus

MINT EDITIONS

The Eumenides was first published in 458 BC.

This edition published by Mint Editions 2020.

ISBN 9781513270326 | E-ISBN 9781513275321

Published by Mint Editions®

MINT
EDITIONS

minteditionbooks.com

Publishing Director: Jennifer Newens
Design & Production: Rachel Lopez Metzger
Translated by: E.D.A. MORSHEAD
Project Manager: Micaela Clark
Typesetting: Westchester Publishing Services

Dramatis Personae

The Pythian Priestess
Apollo
Orestes
The Ghost of Clytemnestra
Chorus of Furies
Athena
Attendants of Athena
Twelve Athenian Citizens

The Scene of the Drama is the Temple of Apollo, at Delphi: afterwards the
Temple of Athena, on the Acropolis of Athens, and the adjoining Areopagus.
The Temple at Delphi

THE PYTHIAN PRIESTESS: First, in this prayer, of all the gods
    I name
   The prophet-mother Earth; and Themis next,
   Second who sat—for so with truth is said—
   On this her mother's shrine oracular.
   Then by her grace, who unconstrained allowed,
   There sat thereon another child of Earth—
   Titanian Phoebe. She, in after time,
   Gave o'er the throne, as birthgift to a god,
   Phoebus, who in his own bears Phoebe's name.
   He from the lake and ridge of Delos' isle
   Steered to the port of Pallas' Attic shores,
   The home of ships; and thence he passed and came
   Unto this land and to Parnassus' shrine.
   And at his side, with awe revering him,
   There went the children of Hephaestus' seed,
   The hewers of the sacred way, who tame
   The stubborn tract that erst was wilderness.
   And all this folk, and Delphos, chieftain-king
   Of this their land, with honour gave him home;
   And in his breast Zeus set a prophet's soul,
   And gave to him this throne, whereon he sits,
   Fourth prophet of the shrine, and, Loxias hight,
   Gives voice to that which Zeus his sire decrees.

   Such gods I name in my preluding prayer,
   And after them, I call with honour due
   On Pallas, wardress of the fane, and Nymphs
   Who dwell around the rock Corycian,
   Where in the hollow cave, the wild birds' haunt,
   Wander the feet of lesser gods; and there,
   Right well I know it, Bromian Bacchus dwells,
   Since he in godship led his Maenad host,
   Devising death for Pentheus, whom they rent
   Piecemeal, as hare among the hounds. And last,

I call on Pleistus' springs, Poseidon's might,
And Zeus most high, the great Accomplisher.
Then as a seeress to the sacred chair
I pass and sit; and may the powers divine
Make this mine entrance fruitful in response
Beyond each former advent, triply blest.
And if there stand without, from Hellas bound,
Men seeking oracles, let each pass in
In order of the lot, as use allows;
For the god guides whate'er my tongue proclaims.

(*She goes into the interior of the temple; after a short interval, she returns in great fear*)

Things fell to speak of, fell for eyes to see,
Have sped me forth again from Loxias' shrine,
With strength unstrung, moving erect no more,
But aiding with my hands my failing feet,
Unnerved by fear. A beldame's force is naught—
Is as a child's, when age and fear combine.
For as I pace towards the inmost fane
Bay-filleted by many a suppliant's hand,
Lo, at the central altar I descry
One crouching as for refuge—yea, a man
Abhorredd of heaven; and from his hands, wherein
A sword new drawn he holds, blood reeked and fell:
A wand he bears, the olive's topmost bough,
Twined as of purpose with a deep close tuft
Of whitest wool. This, that I plainly saw,
Plainly I tell. But lo, in front of him,
Crouched on the altar-steps, a grisly band
Of women slumbers—not like women they,
But Gorgons rather; nay, that word is weak,
Nor may I match the Gorgons' shape with theirs!
Such have I seen in painted semblance erst—
Winged Harpies, snatching food from Phineus' board,—
But these are wingless, black, and all their shape
The eye's abomination to behold.
Fell is the breath—let none draw nigh to it—
Wherewith they snort in slumber; from their eyes
Exude the damnèd drops of poisonous ire:

And such their garb as none should dare to bring
To statues of the gods or homes of men.
I wot not of the tribe wherefrom can come
So fell a legion, nor in what land Earth
Could rear, unharmed, such creatures, nor avow
That she had travailed and brought forth death.
But, for the rest, be all these things a care
Unto the mighty Loxias, the lord
Of this our shrine: healer and prophet he,
Discerner he of portents, and the cleanser
Of other homes—behold, his own to cleanse!

(*Exit*)

(*The scene opens, disclosing the interior of the temple: Orestes clings to the central altar; the Furies lie slumbering at a little distance; Apollo and Hermes appear from the innermost shrine*)

APOLLO: Lo, I desert thee never: to the end,
Hard at thy side as now, or sundered far,
I am thy guard, and to thine enemies
Implacably oppose me: look on them,
These greedy fiends, beneath my craft subdued!
See, they are fallen on sleep, these beldames old,
Unto whose grim and wizened maidenhood
Nor god nor man nor beast can e'er draw near.
Yea, evil were they born, for evil's doom,
Evil the dark abyss of Tartarus
Wherein they dwell, and they themselves the hate
Of men on earth, and of Olympian gods.
But thou, flee far and with unfaltering speed;
For they shall hunt thee through the mainland wide
Where'er throughout the tract of travelled earth
Thy foot may roam, and o'er and o'er the seas
And island homes of men. Faint not nor fail,
Too soon and timidly within thy breast
Shepherding thoughts forlorn of this thy toil;
But unto Pallas' city go, and there
Crouch at her shrine, and in thine arms enfold
Her ancient image: there we well shall find
Meet judges for this cause and suasive pleas,
Skilled to contrive for thee deliverance

From all this woe. Be such my pledge to thee,
For by my hest thou didst thy mother slay.

ORESTES: O king Apollo, since right well thou know'st
What justice bids, have heed, fulfil the same,—
Thy strength is all-sufficient to achieve.

APOLLO: Have thou too heed, nor let thy fear prevail
Above thy will. And do thou guard him, Hermes,
Whose blood is brother unto mine, whose sire
The same high God. Men call thee guide and guard,
Guide therefore thou and guard my suppliant;
For Zeus himself reveres the outlaw's right,
Boon of fair escort, upon man conferred.

(*Exeunt Apollo, Hermes, and Orestes. The Ghost of Clytemnestra near*)

GHOST OF CLYTEMNESTRA: Sleep on! awake! what skills your sleep to
me—
Me, among all the dead by you dishonoured—
Me from whom never, in the world of death,
Dieth this curse, *'Tis she who smote and slew*,
And shamed and scorned I roam? Awake, and hear
My plaint of dead men's hate intolerable.
Me, sternly slain by them that should have loved,
Me doth no god arouse him to avenge,
Hewn down in blood by matricidal hands.
Mark ye these wounds from which the heart's blood ran,
And by whose hand, bethink ye! for the sense
When shut in sleep hath then the spirit-sight,
But in the day the inward eye is blind.
List, ye who drank so oft with lapping tongue
The wineless draught by me outpoured to soothe
Your vengeful ire! how oft on kindled shrine
I laid the feast of darkness, at the hour
Abhorred of every god but you alone!
Lo, all my service trampled down and scorned!
And he hath baulked your chase, as stag the hounds;
Yea, lightly bounding from the circling toils,
Hath wried his face in scorn, and flieth far.
Awake and hear—for mine own soul I cry—
Awake, ye powers of hell! the wandering ghost
That once was Clytemnestra calls—Arise!

(*The Furies mutter grimly, as in a dream*)

> Mutter and murmur! He hath flown afar—My kin have gods to
>   guard them, I have none!

(*The Furies mutter as before*)

> O drowsed in sleep too deep to heed my pain!
> Orestes flies, who me, his mother, slew.

(*The Furies give a confused cry*)

> Yelping, and drowsed again? Up and be doing
> That which alone is yours, the deed of hell!

(*The Furies give another cry*)

> Lo, sleep and toil, the sworn confederates,
> Have quelled your dragon-anger, once so fell!

THE FURIES: (*muttering more fiercely and loudly*) Seize, seize, seize,
    seize—mark, yonder!

GHOST: In dreams ye chase a prey, and like some hound,
> That even in sleep doth ply his woodland toil,
> Ye bell and bay. What do ye, sleeping here?
> Be not o'ercome with toil, nor sleep-subdued,
> Be heedless of my wrong. Up! thrill your heart
> With the just chidings of my tongue,—such words
> Are as a spur to purpose firmly held.
> Blow forth on him the breath of wrath and blood,
> Scorch him with reek of fire that burns in you,
> Waste him with new pursuit—swift, hound him down!

(*Ghost sinks*)

FIRST FURY: (*awaking*) Up! rouse another as I rouse thee; up!
> Sleep'st thou? Rise up, and spurning sleep away,
> See we if false to us this prelude rang.

CHORUS OF FURIES: Alack, alack, O sisters, we have toiled,
>   O much and vainly have we toiled and borne!
> Vainly! and all we wrought the gods have foiled,
>   And turnèd us to scorn!
> He hath slipped from the net, whom we chased: he hath 'scaped us
>   who should be our prey—
> O'ermastered by slumber we sank, and our quarry hath stolen away!
> Thou, child of the high God Zeus, Apollo, hast robbed us and
>   wronged;
> Thou, a youth, hast down-trodden the right that is godship more
>   ancient belonged;

Thou hast cherished thy suppliant man; the slayer the God-forsaken,
The bane of a parent, by craft from out of our grasp thou hast taken:
A god, thou hast stolen from us the avengers a matricide son—
And who shall consider thy deed and say, *It is rightfully* done?

    The sound of chiding scorn
    Came from the land of dream;
Deep to mine inmost heart I felt it thrill and burn,
    Thrust as a strong-grasped goad, to urge
    Onward the chariot's team.
    Thrilled, chilled with bitter inward pain
I stand as one beneath the doomsman's scourge.
Shame on the younger gods who tread down right,
    Sitting on thrones of might!
Woe on the altar of earth's central fane!
    Clotted on step and shrine,
Behold, the guilt of blood, the ghastly stain!
    Woe upon thee, Apollo! uncontrolled,
    Unbidden, hast thou, prophet-god, imbrued
    The pure prophetic shrine with wrongful blood!
    For thou too heinous a respect didst hold
Of man, too little heed of powers divine!
    And us the Fates, the ancients of the earth,
    Didst deem as nothing worth.
Scornful to me thou art, yet shalt not fend
    My wrath from him; though unto hell he flee,
    There too are we!
And he the blood defiled, should feel and rue,
Though I were not, fiend-wrath that shall not end,
Descending on his head who foully slew.

(Re-enter Apollo from the inner shrine)

APOLLO: Out! I command you. Out from this my home—
    Haste, tarry not! Out from the mystic shrine,
    Lest thy lot be to take into thy breast
    The winged bright dart that from my golden string
    Speeds hissing as a snake,—lest, pierced and thrilled
    With agony, thou shouldst spew forth again
    Black frothy heart's-blood, drawn from mortal men,
    Belching the gory clots sucked forth from wounds.
    These be no halls where such as you can prowl—

Go where men lay on men the doom of blood,
Heads lopped from necks, eyes from their spheres plucked out,
Hacked flesh, the flower of youthful seed crushed out,
Feet hewn away, and hands, and death beneath
The smiting stone, low moans and piteous
Of men impaled—Hark, hear ye for what feast
Ye hanker ever, and the loathing gods
Do spit upon your craving? Lo, your shape
Is all too fitted to your greed; the cave
Where lurks some lion, lapping gore, were home
More meet for you. Avaunt from sacred shrines,
Nor bring pollution by your touch on all
That nears you. Hence! and roam unshepherded—
No god there is to tend such herd as you.
CHORUS: O king Apollo, in our turn hear us.
    Thou hast'not only part in these ill things,
    But art chief cause and doer of the same.
APOLLO: How? stretch thy speech to tell this, and have done.
CHORUS: Thine oracle bade this man slay his mother.
APOLLO: I bade him quit his sire's death,—wherefore not?
CHORUS: Then didst thou aid and guard red-handed crime.
APOLLO: Yea, and I bade him to this temple flee.
CHORUS: And yet forsooth dost chide us following him!
APOLLO: Ay—not for you it is, to near this fane.
CHORUS: Yet is such office ours, imposed by fate.
APOLLO: What office? vaunt the thing ye deem so fair.
CHORUS: From home to home we chase the matricide.
APOLLO: What? to avenge a wife who slays her lord?
CHORUS: That is not blood outpoured by kindred hands.
APOLLO: How darkly ye dishonour and annul
    The troth to which the high accomplishers,
    Hera and Zeus, do honour. Yea, and thus
    Is Aphrodite to dishonour cast,
    The queen of rapture unto mortal men.
    Know, that above the marriage-bed ordained
    For man and woman standeth Right as guard,
    Enhancing sanctity of troth-plight sworn;
    Therefore, if thou art placable to those
    Who have their consort slain, nor will'st to turn

On them the eye of wrath, unjust art thou
In hounding to his doom the man who slew
His mother. Lo, I know thee full of wrath
Against one deed, but all too placable
Unto the other, minishing the crime.
But in this cause shall Pallas guard the right.

CHORUS: Deem not my quest shall ever quit that man.

APOLLO: Follow then, make thee double toil in vain!

CHORUS: Think not by speech mine office to curtail.

APOLLO: None hast thou, that I would accept of thee!

CHORUS: Yea, high thine honour by the throne of Zeus:
But I, drawn on by scent of mother's blood,
Seek vengeance on this man and hound him down.

APOLLO: But I will stand beside him; 'tis for me
To guard my suppliant: gods and men alike
Do dread the curse of such an one betrayed,
And in me Fear and Will say *Leave him not*.

(*Exeunt omnes*

The scene changes to Athens. In the foreground, the Temple of Athena on the Acropolis; her statue stands in the centre; Orestes is seen clinging to it)

ORESTES: Look on me, queen Athena; lo, I come
By Loxias' behest; thou of thy grace
Receive me, driven of avenging powers—
Not now a red-hand slayer unannealed,
But with guilt fading, half-effaced, outworn
On many homes and paths of mortal men.
For to the limit of each land, each sea,
I roamed, obedient to Apollo's hest,
And come at last, O Goddess, to thy fane,
And clinging to thine image, bide my doom.

(*Enter the Chorus of Furies, questing like hounds*)

CHORUS: Ho! clear is here the trace of him we seek:
Follow the track of blood, the silent sign!
Like to some hound that hunts a wounded fawn,
We snuff along the scent of dripping gore,
And inwardly we pant, for many a day
Toiling in chase that shall fordo the man;
For o'er and o'er the wide land have I ranged,
And o'er the wide sea, flying without wings,

Swift as a sail I pressed upon his track,
Who now hard by is crouching, well I wot,
For scent of mortal blood allures me here.
    Follow, seek him—round and round
Scent and snuff and scan the ground,
Lest unharmed he slip away,
    He who did his mother slay!
Hist—he is there! See him his arms entwine
Around the image of the maid divine—
    Thus aided, for the deed he wrought
Unto the judgment wills he to be brought.

It may not be! a mother's blood, poured forth
    Upon the stainèd earth,
None gathers up: it lies—bear witness, Hell!—
    For aye indelible!
And thou who sheddest it shalt give thine own
    That shedding to atone!
Yea, from thy living limbs I suck it out,
    Red, clotted, gout by gout,—
A draught abhorred of men and gods; but
    I Will drain it, suck thee dry;
Yea, I will waste thee living, nerve and vein;
    Yea, for thy mother slain,
Will drag thee downward, there where thou shalt dree
    The weird of agony!
And thou and whatsoe'er of men hath sinned—
    Hath wronged or God, or friend,
Or parent,—learn ye how to all and each
    The arm of doom can reach!
Sternly requiteth, in the world beneath,
    The judgment-seat of Death;
Yea, Death, beholding every man's endeavour
Recordeth it for ever.
ORESTES: I, schooled in many miseries, have learnt
    How many refuges of cleansing shrines
    There be; I know when law alloweth speech
    And when imposeth silence. Lo, I stand
    Fixed now to speak, for he whose word is wise

Commands the same. Look, how the stain of blood
Is dull upon mine hand and wastes away,
And laved and lost therewith is the deep curse
Of matricide; for while the guilt was new,
'Twas banished from me at Apollo's hearth,
Atoned and purified by death of swine.
Long were my word if I should sum the tale,
How oft since then among my fellow-men
I stood and brought no curse. Time cleanses all—
Time, the coeval of all things that are.
Now from pure lips, in words of omen fair,
I call Athena, lady of this land,
To come, my champion: so, in aftertime,
She shall not fail of love and service leal,
Not won by war, from me and from my land,
And all the folk of Argos, vowed to her.

    Now, be she far away in Libyan land
Where flows from Triton's lake her natal wave,—
Stand she with planted feet, or in some hour
Of rest conceal them, champion of her friends
Where'er she be,—or whether o'er the plain
Phlegraean she look forth, as warrior bold—
I cry to her to come, where'er she be,
(And she, as goddess, from afar can hear,)
And aid and free me, set among my foes.

CHORUS: Thee not Apollo nor Athena's strength
  Can save from perishing, a castaway
  Amid the Lost, where no delight shall meet
  Thy soul—a bloodless prey of nether powers,
  A shadow among shadows. Answerest thou
  Nothing? dost cast away my words with scorn,
  Thou, prey prepared and dedicate to me?
  Not as a victim slain upon the shrine,
  But living shalt thou see thy flesh my food.
  Hear now the binding chant that makes thee mine.

  Weave the weird dance,—behold the hour
    To utter forth the chant of hell,
    Our sway among mankind to tell,

The guidance of our power.
Of Justice are we ministers,
    And whosoe'er of men may stand
    Lifting a pure unsullied hand,
That man no doom of ours incurs,
    And walks thro' all his mortal path
    Untouched by woe, unharmed by wrath.
    But if, as yonder man, he hath
Blood on the hands he strives to hide,
    We stand avengers at his side,
Decreeing, *Thou hast wronged the dead:*
    We are doom's witnesses to thee.
The price of blood, his hands have shed,
We wring from him; in life, in death,
    Hard at his side are we!

Night, Mother Night, who brought me forth, a torment
    To living men and dead,
Hear me, O hear! by Leto's stripling son
    I am dishonourèd:
He hath ta'en from me him who cowers in refuge,
    To me made consecrate,—
A rightful victim, him who slew his mother.
    Given o'er to me and fate.

    Hear the hymn of hell,
        O'er the victim sounding,—
    Chant of frenzy, chant of ill,
        Sense and will confounding!
    Round the soul entwining
        Without lute or lyre—
    Soul in madness pining,
        Wasting as with fire!

Fate, all-pervading Fate, this service spun, commanding
    That I should bide therein:
Whosoe'er of mortals, made perverse and lawless,
    Is stained with blood of kin,
By his side are we, and hunt him ever onward,

Till to the Silent Land,
The realm of death, he cometh; neither yonder
In freedom shall he stand.

Hear the hymn of hell,
O'er the victim sounding,—
Chant of frenzy, chant of ill,
Sense and will confounding!
Round the soul entwining
Without lute or lyre—
Soul in madness pining,
Wasting as with fire!

When from womb of Night we sprang, on us this labour
Was laid and shall abide.
Gods immortal are ye, yet beware ye touch not
That which is our pride!
None may come beside us gathered round the blood feast—
For us no garments white
Gleam on a festal day; for us a darker fate is,
Another darker rite.
That is mine hour when falls an ancient line—
When in the household's heart
The god of blood doth slay by kindred hands,—
Then do we bear our part:
On him who slays we sweep with chasing cry:
Though he be triply strong,
We wear and waste him; blood atones for blood,
New pain for ancient wrong.

I hold this task—'tis mine, and not another's.
The very gods on high,
Though they can silence and annul the prayers
Of those who on us cry,
They may not strive with us who stand apart,
A race by Zeus abhorred,
Blood-boltered, held unworthy of the council
And converse of Heaven's lord.
Therefore the more I leap upon my prey;

Upon their head I bound;
My foot is hard; as one that trips a runner
I cast them to the ground;
Yea, to the depth of doom intolerable;
And they who erst were great,
And upon earth held high their pride and glory,
Are brought to low estate.
In underworld they waste and are diminished,
The while around them fleet
Dark wavings of my robes, and, subtly woven,
The paces of my feet.

Who falls infatuate, he sees not, neither knows he
That we are at his side;
So closely round about him, darkly flitting,
The cloud of guilt doth glide.
Heavily 'tis uttered, how around his hearthstone
The mirk of hell doth rise.
Stern and fixed the law is; we have hands t'achieve it,
Cunning to devise.
Queens are we and mindful of our solemn vengeance.
Not by tear or prayer
Shall a man avert it. In unhonoured darkness,
Far from gods, we fare,
Lit unto our task with torch of sunless regions,
And o'er a deadly way—
Deadly to the living as to those who see not
    Life and light of day—
Hunt we and press onward. Who of mortals hearing
    Doth not quake for awe,
Hearing all that Fate thro' hand of God hath given us
    For ordinance and law?
Yea, this right to us, in dark abysm and backward
    Of ages it befel:
None shall wrong mine office, tho' in nether regions
    And sunless dark I dwell.
(*Enter Athena from above*)
ATHENA: Far off I heard the clamour of your cry,
    As by Scamander's side I set my foot

Asserting right upon the land given o'er
To me by those who o'er Achaia's host
Held sway and leadership: no scanty part
Of all they won by spear and sword, to me
They gave it, land and all that grew theron,
As chosen heirloom for my Theseus' clan.
Thence summoned, sped I with a tireless foot,—
Hummed on the wind, instead of wings, the fold
Of this mine aegis, by my feet propelled,
As, linked to mettled horses, speeds a car.
And now, beholding here Earth's nether brood,
I fear it nought, yet are mine eyes amazed
With wonder. Who are ye? of all I ask,
And of this stranger to my statue clinging.
But ye—your shape is like no human form,
Like to no goddess whom the gods behold,
Like to no shape which mortal women wear.
Yet to stand by and chide a monstrous form
Is all unjust—from such words Right revolts.

CHORUS: O child of Zeus, one word shall tell thee all.
   We are the children of eternal Night,
   And Furies in the underworld are called.
ATHENA: I know your lineage now and eke your name.
CHORUS: Yea, and eftsoons indeed my rights shalt know.
ATHENA: Fain would I learn them; speak them clearly forth.
CHORUS: We chase from home the murderers of men.
ATHENA: And where at last can he that slew make pause?
CHORUS: Where this is law—*All joy abandon here.*
ATHENA: Say, do ye bay this man to such a flight?
CHORUS: Yea, for of choice he did his mother slay.
ATHENA: Urged by no fear of other wrath and doom?
CHORUS: What spur can rightly goad to matricide?
ATHENA: Two stand to plead—one only have I heard.
CHORUS: He will not swear nor challenge us to oath.
ATHENA: The form of justice, not its deed, thou willest.
CHORUS: Prove thou that word; thou art not scant of skill.
ATHENA: I say that oaths shall not enforce the wrong.
CHORUS: Then test the cause, judge and award the right.
ATHENA: Will ye to me then this decision trust?

CHORUS: Yea, reverencing true child of worthy sire.

ATHENA: (*to Orestes*) O man unknown, make thou thy plea in turn.
Speak forth thy land, thy lineage, and thy woes;
Then, if thou canst, avert this bitter blame—
If, as I deem, in confidence of right
Thou sittest hard beside my holy place,
Clasping this statue, as Ixion sat,
A sacred suppliant for Zeus to cleanse,—
To all this answer me in words made plain.

ORESTES: O queen Athena, first from thy last words
Will I a great solicitude remove.
Not one blood-guilty am I; no foul stain
Clings to thine image from my clinging hand;
Whereof one potent proof I have to tell.
Lo, the law stands—*The slayer shall not plead,*
Till by the hand of him who cleanses blood
A suckling creature's blood besprinkle him.
Long since have I this expiation done,—
In many a home, slain beasts and running streams
Have cleansed me. Thus I speak away that fear.
Next, of my lineage quickly thou shalt learn:
An Argive am I, and right well thou know'st
My sire, that Agamemnon who arrayed
The fleet and them that went therein to war—
That chief with whom thy hand combined to crush
To an uncitied heap what once was Troy;
That Agamemnon, when he homeward came,
Was brought unto no honourable death,
Slain by the dark-souled wife who brought me forth
To him,—enwound and slain in wily nets,
Blazoned with blood that in the laver ran.
And I, returning from an exiled youth,
Slew her, my mother—lo, it stands avowed!
With blood for blood avenging my loved sire;
And in this deed doth Loxias bear part,
Decreeing agonies, to goad my will,
Unless by me the guilty found their doom.
Do thou decide if right or wrong were done—
Thy dooming, whatsoe'er it be, contents me.

ATHENA: Too mighty is this matter, whatsoe'er
     Of mortals claims to judge hereof aright.
     Yea, me, even me, eternal Right forbids
     To judge the issues of blood-guilt, and wrath
     That follows swift behind. This too gives pause,
     That thou as one with all due rites performed
     Dost come, unsinning, pure, unto my shrine.
     Whate'er thou art, in this my city's name,
     As uncondemned, I take thee to my side,—
     Yet have these foes of thine such dues by fate,
     I may not banish them: and if they fail,
     O'erthrown in judgment of the cause, forthwith
     Their anger's poison shall infect the land—
     A dropping plague-spot of eternal ill.
     Thus stand we with a woe on either hand:
     Stay they, or go at my commandment forth,
     Perplexity or pain must needs befall.
     Yet, as on me Fate hath imposed the cause,
     I choose unto me judges that shall be
     An ordinance for ever, set to rule
     The dues of blood-guilt, upon oath declared.
     But ye, call forth your witness and your proof,
     Words strong for justice, fortified by oath;
     And I, whoe'er are truest in my town,
     Them will I chose and bring, and straitly charge,
     Look on this cause, discriminating well,
     And pledge your oath to utter nought of wrong.
(*Exit Athena*)
CHORUS: Now are they all undone, the ancient laws,
          If here the slayer's cause
     Prevail; new wrong for ancient right shall be
          If matricide go free.
     Henceforth a deed like his by all shall stand,
          Too ready to the hand:
     Too oft shall parents in the aftertime
          Rue and lament this crime,—
     Taught, not in false imagining, to feel
          Their children's thrusting steel:
     No more the wrath, that erst on murder fell

From us, the queens of Hell.
Shall fall, no more our watching gaze impend—
    Death shall smite unrestrained.

Henceforth shall one unto another cry
Lo, they are stricken, lo, they fall and die
Around me! and that other answers him,
O thou that lookest that thy woes should cease,
    Behold, with dark increase
They throng and press upon thee; yea, and dim
    Is all the cure, and every comfort vain!

Let none henceforth cry out, when falls the blow
    Of sudden-smiting woe,
      Cry out in sad reiterated strain
    O Justice, aid! aid, O ye thrones of Hell!
So though a father or a mother wail
New-smitten by a son, it shall no more avail,
    Since, overthrown by wrong, the fane of Justice fell!

Know, that a throne there is that may not pass away,
    And one that sitteth on it—even Fear,
Searching with steadfast eyes man's inner soul:
Wisdom is child of pain, and born with many a tear;
    But who henceforth,
What man of mortal men, what nation upon earth,
That holdeth nought in awe nor in the light
Of inner reverence, shall worship Right
    As in the older day?

    Praise not, O man, the life beyond control,
    Nor that which bows unto a tyrant's sway.
      Know that the middle way
Is dearest unto God, and they thereon who wend,
    They shall achieve the end;
    But they who wander or to left or right
    Are sinners in his sight.
    Take to thy heart this one, this soothfast word—
    Of wantonness impiety is sire;

Only from calm control and sanity unstirred
Cometh true weal, the goal of every man's desire.

Yea, whatsoe'er befall, hold thou this word of mine:
Bow down at Justice' shrine,
Turn thou thine eyes away from earthly lure,
Nor with a godless foot that altar spurn.
For as thou dost shall Fate do in return,
And the great doom is sure.
Therefore let each adore a parent's trust,
And each with loyalty revere the guest
That in his halls doth rest.
For whoso uncompelled doth follow what is just,
He ne'er shall be unblest;
Yea, never to the gulf of doom
That man shall come.
But he whose will is set against the gods,
Who treads beyond the law with foot impure,

Till o'er the wreck of Right confusion broods—
Know that for him, though now he sail secure,
The day of storm shall be; then shall he strive and fail,
Down from the shivered yard to furl the sail,
And call on Powers, that heed him nought, to save
And vainly wrestle with the whirling wave,
Hot was his heart with pride—
I shall not fall, he cried.
But him with watching scorn
The god beholds, forlorn,
Tangled in toils of Fate beyond escape,
Hopeless of haven safe beyond the cape—
Till all his wealth and bliss of bygone day
Upon the reef of Rightful Doom is hurled,
And he is rapt away
Unwept, for ever, to the dead forgotten world.
(*Re-enter Athena, with twelve Athenian citizens*)
ATHENA: O herald, make proclaim, bid all men come.
Then let the shrill blast of the Tyrrhene trump,
Fulfilled with mortal breath, thro' the wide air

Peal a loud summons, bidding all men heed.
For, till my judges fill this judgment-seat,
Silence behoves,—that this whole city learn,
What for all time mine ordinance commands,
And these men, that the cause be judged aright.

(*Apollo approaches*)

CHORUS: O king Apollo, rule what is thine own,
But in this thing what share pertains to thee?

APOLLO: First, as a witness come I, for this man
Is suppliant of mine by sacred right,
Guest of my holy hearth and cleansed by me
Of blood-guilt: then, to set me at his side
And in his cause bear part, as part I bore
Erst in his deed, whereby his mother fell.
Let whoso knoweth now announce the cause.

ATHENA: (*to the Chorus*) 'Tis I announce the cause—first speech be yours;
For rightfully shall they whose plaint is tried
Tell the tale first and set the matter clear.

CHORUS: Though we be many, brief shall be our tale.
(*To Orestes*) Answer thou, setting word to match with word;
And first avow—hast thou thy mother slain?

ORESTES: I slew her. I deny no word hereof.

CHORUS: Three falls decide the wrestle—this is one.

ORESTES: Thou vauntest thee—but o'er no final fall.

CHORUS: Yet must thou tell the manner of thy deed.

ORESTES: Drawn sword in hand, I gashed her neck. 'Tis told.

CHORUS: But by whose word, whose craft, wert thou impelled?

ORESTES: By oracles of him who here attests me.

CHORUS: The prophet-god bade thee thy mother slay?

ORESTES: Yea, and thro' him less ill I fared, till now.

CHORUS: If the vote grip thee, thou shalt change that word.

ORESTES: Strong is my hope; my buried sire shall aid.

CHORUS: Go to now, trust the dead, a matricide!

ORESTES: Yea, for in her combined two stains of sin.

CHORUS: How? speak this clearly to the judges' mind.

ORESTES: Slaying her husband, she did slay my sire.

CHORUS: Therefore thou livest; death assoils her deed.

ORESTES: Then while she lived why didst thou hunt her not?

CHORUS: She was not kin by blood to him she slew.

ORESTES: And I, am I by blood my mother's kin?

CHORUS: O cursed with murder's guilt, how else wert thou
    The burden of her womb? Dost thou forswear
    Thy mother's kinship, closest bond of love?

ORESTES: It is thine hour, Apollo—speak the law,
    Averring if this deed were justly done;
    For done it is, and clear and undenied.
    But if to thee this murder's cause seem right
    Or wrongful, speak—that I to these may tell.

APOLLO: To you, Athena's mighty council-court,
    Justly for justice will I plead, even I,
    The prophet-god, nor cheat you by one word.
    For never spake I from my prophet-seat
    One word, of man, of woman, or of state,
    Save what the Father of Olympian gods
    Commanded unto me. I rede you then,
    Bethink you of my plea, how strong it stands,
    And follow the decree of Zeus our sire,—
    For oaths prevail not over Zeus' command.

CHORUS: Go to; thou sayest that from Zeus befel
    The oracle that this Orestes bade
    With vengeance quit the slaying of his sire,
    And hold as nought his mother's right of kin!

APOLLO: Yea, for it stands not with a common death,
    That he should die, a chieftain and a king
    Decked with the sceptre which high heaven confers—
    Die, and by female hands, not smitten down
    By a far-shooting bow, held stalwartly
    By some strong Amazon. Another doom
    Was his: O Pallas, hear, and ye who sit
    In judgment, to discern this thing aright!—
    She with a specious voice of welcome true
    Hailed him, returning from the mighty mart
    Where war for life gives fame, triumphant home;
    Then o'er the laver, as he bathed himself,
    She spread from head to foot a covering net,
    And in the endless mesh of cunning robes
    Enwound and trapped her lord, and smote him down.

Lo, ye have heard what doom this chieftain met,
The majesty of Greece, the fleet's high lord:
Such as I tell it, let it gall your ears,
Who stand as judges to decide this cause.
CHORUS: Zeus, as thou sayest, holds a father's death
As first of crimes,—yet he of his own act
Cast into chains his father, Cronos old:
How suits that deed with that which now ye tell?
O ye who judge, I bid ye mark my words!
APOLLO: O monsters loathed of all, O scorn of gods,
He that hath bound may loose: a cure there is,
Yea, many a plan that can unbind the chain.
But when the thirsty dust sucks up man's blood
Once shed in death, he shall arise no more.
No chant nor charm for this my Sire hath wrought.
All else there is, he moulds and shifts at will,
Not scant of strength nor breath, whate'er he do.
CHORUS: Think yet, for what acquittal thou dost plead:
He who hath shed a mother's kindred blood,
Shall he in Argos dwell, where dwelt his sire?
How shall he stand before the city's shrines,
How share the clansmen's holy lustral bowl?
APOLLO: This too I answer; mark a soothfast word,
Not the true parent is the woman's womb
That bears the child; she doth but nurse the seed
New-sown: the male is parent; she for him,
As stranger for a stranger, hoards the germ
Of life; unless the god its promise blight.
And proof hereof before you will I set.
Birth may from fathers, without mothers, be:
See at your side a witness of the same,
Athena, daughter of Olympian Zeus,
Never within the darkness of the womb
Fostered nor fashioned, but a bud more bright
Than any goddess in her breast might bear.
And I, O Pallas, howsoe'er I may,
Henceforth will glorify thy town, thy clan,
And for this end have sent my suppliant here
Unto thy shrine; that he from this time forth

Be loyal unto thee for evermore,
O goddess-queen, and thou unto thy side
Mayst win and hold him faithful, and his line,
And that for aye this pledge and troth remain
To children's children of Athenian seed.

ATHENA: Enough is said; I bid the judges now
With pure intent deliver just award.

CHORUS: We too have shot our every shaft of speech,
And now abide to hear the doom of law.

ATHENA: (*to Apollo and Orestes*) Say, how ordaining shall I 'scape your
blame?

APOLLO: I spake, ye heard; enough. O stranger men,
Heed well your oath as ye decide the cause.

ATHENA: O men of Athens, ye who first do judge
The law of bloodshed, hear me now ordain.
Here to all time for Aegeus' Attic host
Shall stand this council-court of judges sworn,
Here the tribunal, set on Ares' Hill
Where camped of old the tented Amazons,
What time in hate of Theseus they assailed
Athens, and set against her citadel
A counterwork of new sky-pointing towers,
And there to Ares held their sacrifice,
Where now the rock hath name, even Ares' Hill.
And hence shall Reverence and her kinsman Fear
Pass to each free man's heart, by day and night
Enjoining, *Thou shalt do no unjust thing*,
So long as law stands as it stood of old
Unmarred by civic change. Look you, the spring
Is pure; but foul it once with influx vile
And muddy clay, and none can drink thereof.
Therefore, O citizens, I bid ye bow
In awe to this command, *Let no man live*
Uncurbed by law nor curbed by tyranny;
Nor banish ye the monarchy of Awe
Beyond the walls; untouched by fear divine,
No man doth justice in the world of men.
Therefore in purity and holy dread
Stand and revere; so shall ye have and hold

A saving bulwark of the state and land,
Such as no man hath ever elsewhere known,
Nor in far Scythia, nor in Pelops' realm.
Thus I ordain it now, a council-court
Pure and unsullied by the lust of gain,
Sacred and swift to vengeance, wakeful ever
To champion men who sleep, the country's guard.
Thus have I spoken, thus to mine own clan
Commended it for ever. Ye who judge,
Arise, take each his vote, mete out the right,
Your oath revering. Lo, my word is said.

(The twelve judges come forward, one by one, to the urns of decision; the first votes; as each of the others follows, the Chorus and Apollo speak alternately)

CHORUS: I rede ye well, beware! nor put to shame,
In aught, this grievous company of hell.

APOLLO: I too would warn you, fear mine oracles—
From Zeus they are,—nor make them void of fruit.

CHORUS: Presumptuous is thy claim, blood-guilt to judge,
And false henceforth thine oracles shall be.

APOLLO: Failed then the counsels of my sire, when turned
Ixion, first of slayers, to his side?

CHORUS: These are but words; but I, if justice fail me,
Will haunt this land in grim and deadly deed.

APOLLO: Scorn of the younger and the elder gods
Art thou: 'tis I that shall prevail anon.

CHORUS: Thus didst thou too of old in Pheres' halls,
O'erreaching Fate to make a mortal deathless.

APOLLO: Was it not well, my worshipper to aid,
Then most of all when hardest was the need?

CHORUS: I say thou didst annul the lots of life,
Cheating with wine the deities of eld.

APOLLO: I say thou shalt anon, thy pleadings foiled,
Spit venom vainly on thine enemies.

CHORUS: Since this young god o'errides mine ancient right,
I tarry but to claim your law, not knowing
If wrath of mine shall blast your state or spare

ATHENA: Mine is the right to add the final vote,
And I award it to Orestes' cause.

For me no mother bore within her womb,
And, save for wedlock evermore eschewed,
I vouch myself the champion of the man,
Not of the woman, yea, with all my soul,—
In heart, as birth, a father's child alone.
Thus will I not too heinously regard
A woman's death who did her husband slay,
The guardian of her home; and if the votes
Equal do fall, Orestes shall prevail.
Ye of the judges who are named thereto,
Swiftly shake forth the lots from either urn.

(*Two judges come forward, one to each urn*)

ORESTES: O bright Apollo, what shall be the end?
CHORUS: O Night, dark mother mine, dost mark these things?
OSESTES: Now shall my doom be life, or strangling cords.
CHORUS: And mine, lost honour or a wider sway.
APOLLO: O stranger judges, sum aright the count
    Of votes cast forth, and, parting them, take heed
    Ye err not in decision. The default
    Of one vote only bringeth ruin deep,
    One, cast aright, doth stablish house and home.
ATHENA: Behold, this man is free from guilt of blood,
    For half the votes condemn him, half set free!
ORESTES: O Pallas, light and safety of my home,
    Thou, thou hast given me back to dwell once more
    In that my fatherland, amerced of which
    I wandered; now shall Grecian lips say this,
    The man is Argive once again, and dwells
    Again within his father's wealthy hall,
    By Pallas saved, by Loxias, and by Him,
    The great third saviour, Zeus omnipotent—
    Who thus in pity for my father's fate
    Doth pluck me from my doom, beholding these,
    Confederates of my mother. Lo, I pass
    To mine own home, but proffering this vow
    Unto thy land and people: *Nevermore,*
    Thro' all the manifold years of Time to be,
    Shall any chieftain of mine Argive land
    Bear hitherward his spears for fight arrayed.

For we, though lapped in earth we then shall lie,
By thwart adversities will work our will
On them who shall transgress this oath of mine,
Paths of despair and journeyings ill-starred
For them ordaining, till their task they rue.
But if this oath be rightly kept, to them
Will we the dead be full of grace, the while
With loyal league they honour Pallas' town.
And now farewell, thou and thy city's folk—
Firm be thine arm's grasp, closing with thy foes,
And, strong to save, bring victory to thy spear.

(*Exit Orestes, with Apollo*)

CHORUS: Woe on you, younger gods! the ancient right
    Ye have o'erridden, rent it from my hands.

I am dishonoured of you, thrust to scorn!
    But heavily my wrath
Shall on this land fling forth the drops that blast and burn
    Venom of vengeance, that shall work such scathe
    As I have suffered; where that dew shall fall,
      Shall leafless blight arise,
    Wasting Earth's offspring,—Justice, hear my call!—
    And thorough all the land in deadly wise
    Shall scatter venom, to exude again
      In pestilence on men.
    What cry avails me now, what deed of blood,
    Unto this land what dark despite?
      Alack, alack, forlorn
    Are we, a bitter injury have borne!
    Alack, O sisters, O dishonoured brood
      Of mother Night!

ATHENA: Nay, bow ye to my words, chafe not nor moan:
    Ye are not worsted nor disgraced; behold,
    With balanced vote the cause had issue fair,
    Nor in the end did aught dishonour thee.
    But thus the will of Zeus shone clearly forth,
    And his own prophet-god avouched the same,
    Orestes slew: his slaying is atoned.
    Therefore I pray you, not upon this land

Shoot forth the dart of vengeance; be appeased,
Nor blast the land with blight, nor loose thereon
Drops of eternal venom, direful darts
Wasting and marring nature's seed of growth.

For I, the queen of Athens' sacred right,
Do pledge to you a holy sanctuary
Deep in the heart of this my land, made just
By your indwelling presence, while ye sit
Hard by your sacred shrines that gleam with oil
Of sacrifice, and by this folk adored.

CHORUS: Woe on you, younger gods! the ancient right
Ye have o'erridden, rent it from my hands.

I am dishonoured of you, thrust to scorn!
    But heavily my wrath
Shall on his land fling forth the drops that blast and burn.
    Venom of vengeance, that shall work such scathe
    As I have suffered; where that dew shall fall,
       Shall leafless blight arise,
Wasting Earth's offspring,—Justice, hear my call!—
And thorough all the land in deadly wise
Shall scatter venom, to exude again
    In pestilence of men.
What cry avails me now, what deed of blood,
Unto this land what dark despite?
    Alack, alack, forlorn
Are we, a bitter injury have borne!
Alack, O sisters, O dishonoured brood
    Of mother Night!

ATHENA: Dishonoured are ye not; turn not, I pray,
As goddesses your swelling wrath on men,
Nor make the friendly earth despiteful to them.
I too have Zeus for champion—'tis enough—
I only of all goddesses do know.
To ope the chamber where his thunderbolts
Lie stored and sealed; but here is no such need.
Nay, be appeased, nor cast upon the ground
The malice of thy tongue, to blast the world;

Calm thou thy bitter wrath's black inward surge,
For high shall be thine honour, set beside me
For ever in this land, whose fertile lap
Shall pour its teeming firstfruits unto you,
Gifts for fair childbirth and for wedlock's crown:
Thus honoured, praise my spoken pledge for aye.

CHORUS: I, I dishonoured in this earth to dwell,—
Ancient of days and wisdom! I breathe forth
Poison and breath of frenzied ire. O Earth,
    Woe, woe, for thee, for me!
From side to side what pains be these that thrill?
Hearken, O mother Night, my wrath, mine agony!
Whom from mine ancient rights the gods have thrust,
    And brought me to the dust—
Woe, woe is me!—with craft invincible.

ATHENA: Older art thou than I, and I will bear
With this thy fury. Know, although thou be
More wise in ancient wisdom, yet have I
From Zeus no scanted measure of the same,
Wherefore take heed unto this prophecy—
If to another land of alien men
Ye go, too late shall ye feel longing deep
For mine. The rolling tides of time bring round
A day of brighter glory for this town;
And thou, enshrined in honour by the halls
Where dwelt Erechtheus, shalt a worship win
From men and from the train of womankind,
Greater than any tribe elsewhere shall pay.
Cast thou not therefore on this soil of mine
Whetstones that sharpen souls to bloodshedding.
The burning goads of youthful hearts, made hot
With frenzy of the spirit, not of wine.
Nor pluck as 'twere the heart from cocks that strive,
To set it in the breasts of citizens
Of mine, a war-god's spirit, keen for fight,
Made stern against their country and their kin.
The man who grievously doth lust for fame,
War, full, immitigable, let him wage
Against the stranger; but of kindred birds

I hold the challenge hateful. Such the boon
I proffer thee—within this land of lands,
Most loved of gods, with me to show and share
Fair mercy, gratitude and grace as fair.

CHORUS: I, I dishonoured in this earth to dwell,—
Ancient of days and wisdom! I breathe forth
Poison and breath of frenzied ire. O Earth,
    Woe, woe for thee, for me!
From side to side what pains be these that thrill?
Hearken, O mother Night, my wrath, mine agony!
Whom from mine ancient rights the gods have thrust,
    And brought me to the dust—
Woe, woe is me!—with craft invincible.

ATHENA: I will not weary of soft words to thee,
That never mayst thou say, *Behold me spurned,*
An elder by a younger deity,
And from this land rejected and forlorn,
Unhonoured by the men who dwell therein.
But, if Persuasion's grace be sacred to thee,
Soft in the soothing accents of my tongue,
Tarry, I pray thee; yet, if go thou wilt,
Not rightfully wilt thou on this my town
Sway down the scale that beareth wrath and teen
Or wasting plague upon this folk. 'Tis thine,
If so thou wilt, inheritress to be
Of this my land, its utmost grace to win.

CHORUS: O queen, what refuge dost thou promise me?
ATHENA: Refuge untouched by bale: take thou my boon.
CHORUS: What, if I take it, shall mine honour be?
ATHENA: No house shall prosper without grace of thine.
CHORUS: Canst thou achieve and grant such power to me?
ATHENA: Yea, for my hand shall bless thy worshippers.
CHORUS: And wilt thou pledge me this for time eterne?
ATHENA: Yea: none can bid me pledge beyond my power.
CHORUS: Lo, I desist from wrath, appeased by thee.
ATHENA: Then in the land's heart shalt thou win thee friends.
CHORUS: What chant dost bid me raise, to greet the land?
ATHENA: Such as aspires towards a victory
Unrued by any: chants from breast of earth,

From wave, from sky; and let the wild winds' breath
Pass with soft sunlight o'er the lap of land,—
Strong wax the fruits of earth, fair teem the kine,
Unfailing, for my town's prosperity,
And constant be the growth of mortal seed.
But more and more root out the impious,
For as a gardener fosters what he sows,
So foster I this race, whom righteousness
Doth fend from sorrow. Such the proffered boon.
But I, if wars must be, and their loud clash
And carnage, for my town, will ne'er endure
That aught but victory shall crown her fame.
Chorus: Lo, I accept it; at her very side
   Doth Pallas bid me dwell:
  I will not wrong the city of her pride,
Which even Almighty Zeus and Ares hold
   Heaven's earthly citadel,
 Loved home of Grecian gods, the young, the old,
   The sanctuary divine,
   The shield of every shrine!
For Athens I say forth a gracious prophecy,—
  The glory of the sunlight and the skies
   Shall bid from earth arise
Warm wavelets of new life and glad prosperity.
Athena: Behold, with gracious heart well pleased
   I for my citizens do grant
   Fulfilment of this covenant:
And here, their wrath at length appeased,
   These mighty deities shall stay,
  For theirs it is by right to sway
The lot that rules our mortal day,
    And he who hath not inly felt
   Their stern decree, ere long on him,
   Not knowing why and whence, the grim
    Life-crushing blow is dealt.
    The father's sin upon the child
   Descends, and sin is silent death,
   And leads him on the downward path,
    By stealth beguiled,

Unto the Furies: though his state
On earth were high, and loud his boast,
Victim of silent ire and hate
He dwells among the Lost.

CHORUS: To my blessing now give ear.—
Scorching blight nor singèd air
Never blast thine olives fair!
Drouth, that wasteth bud and plant,
Keep to thine own place. Avaunt,
Famine fell, and come not hither
Stealthily to waste and wither!
Let the land, in season due,
Twice her waxing fruits renew;
Teem the kine in double measure;
Rich in new god-given treasure;
Here let men the powers adore
For sudden gifts unhoped before!

ATHENA: O hearken, warders of the wall
That guards mine Athens, what a dower
Is unto her ordained and given!
For mighty is the Furies' power,
And deep-revered in courts of heaven
And realms of hell; and clear to all
They weave thy doom, mortality!
And some in joy and peace shall sing;
But unto other some they bring
Sad life and tear-dimmed eye.

CHORUS: And far away I ban thee and remove,
Untimely death of youths too soon brought low!
And to each maid, O gods, when time is come for love,
Grant ye a warrior's heart, a wedded life to know.
Ye too, O Fates, children of mother Night,
Whose children too are we, O goddesses
Of just award, of all by sacred right
Queens who in time and in eternity
Do rule, a present power for righteousness,
Honoured beyond all Gods, hear ye and grant my cry!

ATHENA: And I too, I with joy am fain,
Hearing your voice this gift ordain

Unto my land. High thanks be thine,
Persuasion, who with eyes divine
Into my tongue didst look thy strength,
     To bend and to appease at length
Those who would not be comforted.
     Zeus, king of parley, doth prevail,
And ye and I will strive nor fail,
     That good may stand in evil's stead,
And lasting bliss for bale.
CHORUS: And nevermore these walls within
     Shall echo fierce sedition's din
          Unslaked with blood and crime;
     The thirsty dust shall nevermore
     Suck up the darkly streaming gore
     Of civic broils, shed out in wrath
     And vengeance, crying death for death!
     But man with man and state with state
     Shall vow *The pledge of common hate*
     And common friendship, that for man
     Hath oft made blessing out of ban,
     Be ours unto all time.
ATHENA: Skill they, or not, the path to find
     Of favouring speech and presage kind?
     Yea, even from these, who, grim and stern,
          Glared anger upon you of old,
     O citizens, ye now shall earn
          A recompense right manifold.
     Deck them aright, extol them high,
     Be loyal to their loyalty,
          And ye shall make your town and land
          Sure, propped on Justice' saving hand,
     And Fame's eternity.
CHORUS: Hail ye, all hail! and yet again, all hail
          O Athens, happy in a weal secured!
     O ye who sit by Zeus' right hand, nor fail
          Of wisdom set among you and assured,
     Loved of the well-loved Goddess-Maid! the King
     Of gods doth reverence you, beneath her guarding
          wing.

ATHENA: All hail unto each honoured guest!
    Whom to the chambers of your rest
    'Tis mine to lead, and to provide
    The hallowed torch, the guard and guide.
    Pass down, the while these altars glow
    With sacred fire, to earth below
       And your appointed shrine.
    There dwelling, from the land restrain
    The force of fate, the breath of bane,
    But waft on us the gift and gain
       Of Victory divine!
    And ye, the men of Cranaos' seed,
    I bid you now with reverence lead
    These alien Powers that thus are made
    Athenian evermore. To you
    Fair be their will henceforth, to do
       Whate'er may bless and aid!
CHORUS: Hail to you all! hail yet again,
    All who love Athens, Gods and men,
       Adoring her as Pallas' home!
    And while ye reverence what ye grant—
    My sacred shrine and hidden haunt—
       Blameless and blissful be your doom!
ATHENA: Once more I praise the promise of your vows,
    And now I bid the golden torches' glow
    Pass down before you to the hidden depth
    Of earth, by mine own sacred servants borne,
    My loyal guards of statue and of shrine.
    Come forth, O flower of Theseus' Attic land,
    O glorious band of children and of wives,
    And ye, O train of matrons crowned with eld!
    Deck you with festal robes of scarlet dye
    In honour of this day: O gleaming torch,
    Lead onward, that these gracious powers of earth
    Henceforth be seen to bless the life of men.
(*Athena leads the procession downwards into the Cave of the Furies, under Areopagus: as they go, the escort of women and children chant aloud*)
CHANT: With loyalty we lead you; proudly go,
    Night's childless children, to your home below!

(*O citizens, awhile from words forbear!*)
To darkness' deep primeval lair,
Far in Earth's bosom, downward fare,
Adored with prayer and sacrifice.
 (*O citizens, forbear your cries!*)
Pass hitherward, ye powers of Dread,
With all your former wrath allayed,
 Into the heart of this loved land;
With joy unto your temple wend,
The while upon your steps attend
 The flames that fed upon the brand—
(*Now, now ring out your chant, your joy's acclaim!*)
 Behind them, as they downward fare,
 Let holy hands libations bear,
  And torches' sacred flame.
 All-seeing Zeus and Fate come down
  To battle fair for Pallas' town!
 Ring out your chant, ring out your joy's acclaim!
(*Exeunt omnes*)

A Note About the Author

Aeschylus (c. 525–455 B.C.) was an ancient Greek playwright and soldier. Scholars' knowledge of the tragedy genre begins with Aeschylus' work, and because of this, he is dubbed the "father of tragedy." Aeschylus claimed his inspiration to become a writer stemmed from a dream he had in which the god Dionysus encouraged him to write a play. While it is estimated that he wrote just under one hundred plays, only seven of Aeschylus' work was able to be recovered.

A Note from the Publisher

Spanning many genres, from non-fiction essays to literature classics to children's books and lyric poetry, Mint Edition books showcase the master works of our time in a modern new package. The text is freshly typeset, is clean and easy to read, and features a new note about the author in each volume. Many books also include exclusive new introductory material. Every book boasts a striking new cover, which makes it as appropriate for collecting as it is for gift giving. Mint Edition books are only printed when a reader orders them, so natural resources are not wasted. We're proud that our books are never manufactured in excess and exist only in the exact quantity they need to be read and enjoyed.

bookfinity™

Discover more of your favorite classics with Bookfinity™.

- Track your reading with custom book lists.
- Get great book recommendations for your personalized Reader Type.
- Add reviews for your favorite books.
- AND MUCH MORE!

Visit **bookfinity.com** and take the fun Reader Type quiz to get started.

Enjoy our classic and modern companion pairings!